NEVILLE

For I.C. with admiration and thanks—N.J.

For Alexander Shundi, a teacher like no other—G.B.K.

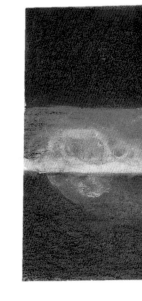

Library of Congress Cataloging-in-Publication Data

Juster, Norton.

Neville / Norton Juster ; [illustrations by G. Brian Karas].—1st ed.

p. cm.

Summary: When a boy and his family move to a new house, he devises an
ingenious way to meet people in the neighborhood.

ISBN 978-0-375-86765-1 (trade) – ISBN 978-0-375-96765-8 (glb)

[1. Moving, Household—Fiction.] I. Karas, G. Brian, ill. II. Title.

PZ7.J98Ne 2011

[E]—dc22

2010024119

The text of this book is set in Regula.

The illustrations were rendered in mixed media.

MANUFACTURED IN MALAYSIA

10 9 8 7 6 5 4 3 2 1

First Edition

NEVILLE

by NORTON JUSTER

illustrated by G. BRIAN KARAS

schwartz & wade books · new york

The big gray van pulled away from the curb, moved slowly down the street, and disappeared around the corner. Now it was quiet, and there he was, where he really didn't want to be.

Nobody had asked him about moving. They'd just told him.

"You'll love it," they'd said. That's what they always said when they knew he wouldn't love something.

So now he had a new house where he'd never feel at home. And a new school where nobody knew him. "Now, class, here is the new boy I told you about," he imagined the teacher saying. "He comes from the South Pole, and you can all make fun of him as much as you want."

And, of course, there were no friends. That was the worst part, no friends.

The boy sat quite still on the front steps. His mother was standing just inside the doorway. "I know it's hard," she said in her soft mother's voice. "Just give it a chance. I think everything is going to be fine."

He didn't look up.

She came down the four steps and sat next to him. "Maybe you'd like to take a little walk down the block. You might even meet someone."

"Yeah, sure," he mumbled, "like you can make new friends just by walking down the block."

But there wasn't much else to do, so he pulled himself to his feet and slowly shuffled away.

"Don't go too far," his mother cautioned.

"Yeah, sure."

"Watch out for cars if you cross."

"Yeah, sure."

"Come back before it starts to get dark."

"Yeah, sure."

He moved along, looking at the houses without much
interest. When he had almost reached the end of the block,
he stopped and stood perfectly still for a moment, as if he
wasn't sure what he was going to do. Then he turned around
slowly, put his head back, took a deep breath, and called out,

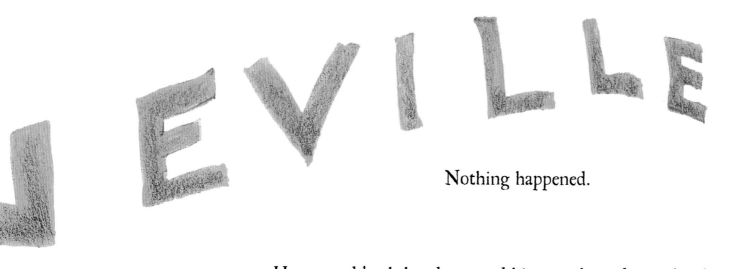

EVILLE

Nothing happened.

He cupped both hands around his mouth, and now he shouted,

NEVILLE

"He probably can't hear you. You have to shout louder,"
came a voice from close by.

A boy just about his size was standing right next to him.

A little startled, he shouted again, even louder,

"NO, NO, NO, still not good. Let's try it together." They both shouted as loud as they could, but not very together,

"That doesn't sound right," said a serious girl who had walked over from the other side of the street. "You have to do it at exactly the same time, or no one will understand you. Here, watch me."

She raised her arms, counted to three and brought them down like a conductor. They all shouted together at exactly the same time,

"Excellent!" said the girl, smiling brightly.

There was still no reply, but more children came trotting up from every direction. It was quite a crowd, and some started shouting before they even got to the group.

It was difficult for them to keep together, especially when several dogs joined in, howling, but everyone enjoyed trying.

When they stopped to catch their breath, one of the children said, "Hey, I don't know anyone named Neville who lives around here. Is he new?"

"I guess so," the boy said uncertainly. "Everyone has to be new sometimes, don't they?"

That sounded reasonable. They all nodded.

"Are you a friend of his?" they asked.

"His best friend, I guess," said the boy.

One of the girls said softly, "If Neville likes you so much, you must be special."

"Well, I don't know, maybe a little," he had to admit.

What's Neville like?.

Does he play ball?

When

Does broth siste

Now they gathered around, and their questions came from all sides. Everyone wanted to know more about Neville.

The boy tried to answer the questions as best he could, and everyone seemed very excited to learn more.

Is he smart?

Does he like to read?

move here?

Is he nice? I hope he doesn't push.

Will he come to sleepovers?

Is he funny?

"I like Neville already!"
someone cried out.

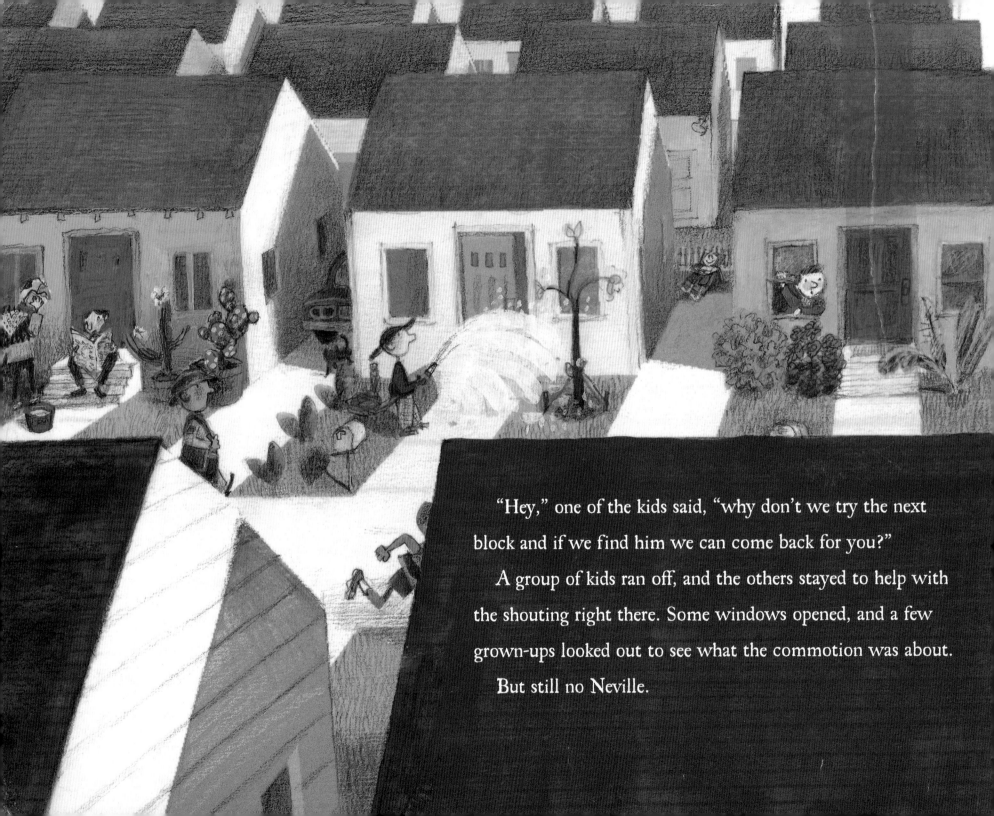

"Hey," one of the kids said, "why don't we try the next block and if we find him we can come back for you?"

A group of kids ran off, and the others stayed to help with the shouting right there. Some windows opened, and a few grown-ups looked out to see what the commotion was about.

But still no Neville.

"I think I have to go," said one of the girls after a while, "or my mother will get all bothered."

"I guess I have to go too," the boy said quietly.

"Can we come back tomorrow and help some more?" the kids asked. "Will you come?"

"Are you sure?"

"PROMISE!"

"Sure, if you want," he agreed, and they all began to walk and skip away.

For a few seconds the boy stood quietly watching
and listening to what they were saying.

I hope we find Neville.

Even if we don't, I like his friend a lot.

MaYBE BETTER!

HEY, what was his name?

Oh, we'll have to ask him tomorrow.

The boy turned and started back toward his new house.

The sun was getting low and the shadows long, and as he got close he looked up at the house.

"Not so bad," he had to admit. He went up the steps two at a time.

The boy had his dinner right away.
Nothing in the house was fixed up yet,
but it didn't bother him.

He washed, got into his pajamas,
and dove into bed.

His mom came to tuck him in.

"Long day," she sighed as she bent to kiss him good night. "I hope you'll like it here."
She turned off the light and walked toward the door.

"Good night, Neville, pleasant dreams," she whispered.

"Good night, Mom," he whispered back, and in a moment he was asleep.